THE KINGS OF COLORING

Coloring enthusiasts! We appreciate your support!
Thank you for buying our book -- we're excited to see your work!
If you're active on social media, please share your art with us!
Our username on all platforms is @tkocofficial -- TAG US!
We would also be very grateful if you left us a review on Amazon

Before you start coloring

In order to provide you with a positive coloring experience
We recommend testing your supplies on our "Color Swatch" page!
This page is included at the back of our books

Tip: If you're using a lot of markers, consider placing a few sheets of
paper behind the page that you're coloring to avoid bleeding
* For best results, we suggest using colored pencils *

HAPPY COLORING

THE KINGS OF COLORING

TKOC

THE KINGS OF COLORING

TKOC

THE KINGS OF COLORING

TKOC

THE KINGS OF COLORING

TKOC

THE KINGS OF COLORING

TKOC

THE KINGS OF COLORING

TKOC

THE KINGS OF COLORING

TKOC

THE KINGS OF COLORING

TKOC

THE KINGS OF COLORING

ZOMBIES IN SPACE

HEAVY METAL

MATTY SHREDS

ALIENS

THANK YOU! WE APPRECIATE YOUR PURCHASE AND SUPPORT!

CHECK OUT SOME SAMPLE PAGES FROM OUR OTHER TITLES!

TKOC

TKOC

THE KINGS OF COLORING

TKOC

THE KINGS OF COLORING

TKOC

THE KINGS OF COLORING

TKOC

THE KINGS OF COLORING

TKOC

THE KINGS OF COLORING

TKOC

THE KINGS OF COLORING

TKOC

THE KINGS OF COLORING

TKOC

THE KINGS OF COLORING

TKOC

THE KINGS OF COLORING

GOT MERCH?!
IF NOT, GO STRENGTHEN YOUR WARDROBE BY VISITING:

WWW.SHOPTKOC.COM

THE KINGS OF COLORING

ZOMBIES
ADULT COLORING BOOK

SILLY MONSTERS
COLORING BOOK

ABSTRACT
ADULT COLORING BOOK

ZOMBIES IN SPACE
ADULT COLORING BOOK

ROBOTS
COLORING BOOK

THE KINGS OF COLORING

SUGAR SKULLS
ADULT COLORING BOOK

ALIENS
ADULT COLORING BOOK

TEDDY BEARS
COLORING BOOK

STAINED GLASS
ADULT COLORING BOOK

SUITS & DRESSES
COLORING BOOK

THE KINGS OF COLORING

MATTY SHREDS
COLORING BOOK

CHRISTMAS
COLORING BOOK

CHRISTMAS II
COLORING BOOK

EYES
COLORING BOOK

HEAVY METAL
ADULT COLORING BOOK

THE KINGS OF COLORING

CRYSTALS & HOROSCOPES
ADULT COLORING BOOK

EVIL ROBOTS
ADULT COLORING BOOK

SKATEBOARDING
COLORING BOOK

FLOWERS
COLORING BOOK

CAKES & DESSERTS
COLORING BOOK

THE KINGS OF COLORING

SKATEBOARD OR DIE

COLLECT THEM ALL !

TKOC

COLOR SWATCHES
TEST YOUR SUPPLIES

THE KINGS OF COLORING

Printed in Great Britain
by Amazon